MW00965987

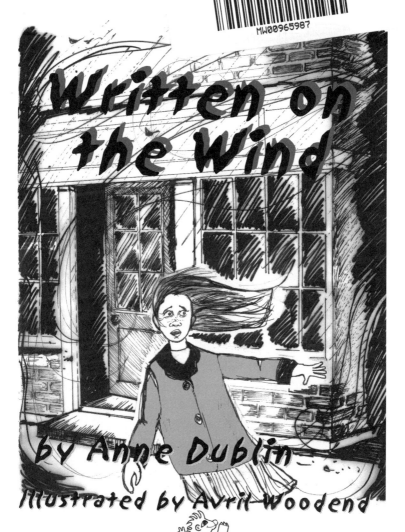

Written on the Wind

by Anne Dublin

Illustrated by Avril Woodend

A Hodgepog Book

Hodgepog Books acknowledges the ongoing support of the Canada
Council for the Arts.

Editors: Luanne Armstrong, Dorothy Woodend & Amanda Gibbs

Cover design by Dorothy Woodend
Inside layout by Linda Uyehara Hoffman
Set in Palatino, Sand and Helvetica in Quark XPress 4.1
Printed at Hignell Book Printing

A Hodgepog Book for Kids

Published in Canada by Hodgepog Books
3476 Tupper Street
Vancouver, BC
V5Z 3B7
Telephone (604) 874-1167
Fax (604) 681-1431
Email: dorothy@axion.net

Canadian Cataloguing in Publication Data

Dublin, Anne
    Written on the Wind

ISBN 0-9686899-5-7

I. Woodend, Avril 1968-11. Title.

PS8557.U233W74 2001 jC813'.6 C2001-911191-6
PZ7.D8497Wr 2001

The Canada Council | Le Conseil des Arts
for the Arts | du Canada

For Max, who was there.

Table of Contents

Chapter One

My teacher, Miss Johnson, says I'll feel better if I write about what happened a week ago. October 15, 1954, to be exact. So I'll try. But I still feel pretty confused about the whole thing. Especially about Evelyn. But I guess I should start at the beginning, before all the trouble began.

I live in a large, three-story house near the corner of Manning Avenue and Palmerston Gardens in downtown Toronto. The elm and maple trees on the street are very tall, standing on tiptoe to touch each other's branches. I like to pretend that the trees are playing "London Bridge is Falling Down", the same way that we girls hold our arms when we play that game during recess.

My parents, my twin brother, Michael, and I live in three rooms on the first floor. There's a kitchen, a front room, and a room that we all sleep in. I think our sleeping room used to be a dining room because it has a big bay window.

I hate being so crowded. When I complain, Mama says, "It used to be much worse. When we first came to Canada, we all had to live together in two rooms on the third floor of an old house on Huron Street. We didn't even have running water. I'd have to go downstairs to get water every time I needed some for cooking or washing.

"Everybody used to complain, 'Why can't you keep your kids quiet? Why do they have to run around so much?' We were really happy when we finally had enough money a few years ago for a down payment for this house."

All I remember about the other house is the huge German shepherd called Rex in the yard on the other side of the lane. I used to be afraid to pass that yard because Rex would start barking and growling and snarling until I was farther down the block. I was glad to move, that's for sure.

Michael says he's glad we moved too. There are more things to do in our neighbourhood and more kids to play with. Mama calls it mischief; Michael calls it fun.

Mama says, "Things are much better now. We have the whole first floor to ourselves and even the basement." Anyway, another family lives on the second floor and a married couple live on the third floor.

Mama says we have to rent out the flats so that Papa can pay off the mortgage. Then we'll be able to have more space when I'm older. I wish I were older now.

The problem is that all three families have to share one bathroom on the second floor. I already know that I shouldn't wait until the last minute to go to the bathroom. Sometimes, after I've been playing outside, I forget. I hurry up to the bathroom and have to wait outside the door.

I knock on the door and shout, "Please hurry up!" but sometimes I get pretty desperate. I have to cross my legs so that I won't go in my pants while I'm waiting. I hate sharing the bathroom with so many people! My friend Myra lives in a big house down the street and she doesn't have to share her bathroom with strangers—only with the other people in her family.

I hate being poor; I hate being an immigrant. I want to fit in with the other kids, to be Canadian like them. I couldn't even speak English when I started kindergarten, just Yiddish that we spoke at home. I'm glad that Michael was there with me in Miss Featherstone's class. I was bawling my head off, I was so scared. Michael couldn't speak English either, but he didn't cry. He's braver than me and stayed with me the whole morning. Now I can speak English, but I still don't fit in.

Mama tries to help but she doesn't understand. I want store-bought clothes, not the homemade, old-fashioned ones that Mama sews. I want to go to a real beauty parlour to get my hair cut, not have Mama cut my hair with the big tailor scissors while I sit on a kitchen chair with a towel on my shoulders.

"Ouch!" I yell, as Mama combs my hair with the fine-toothed metal comb.

"Hold still!" Mama says. "I don't know how your hair gets so tangled all the time!"

Mama and Papa came from Poland after the war. They lost their homes and their families and everything. Papa says, "I had only ten dollars in my pocket when we came to Canada." Then he adds, with a twinkle in his eye, "But we had you and Michael; so we felt rich." I'm glad we live in a safe country, but I still wish we weren't immigrants.

I like how the houses are so close together on our street. There's a narrow little sidewalk between our house and Mr. Malone's next door. Mr. Malone works nights and sleeps days and always gets mad at us kids when we play between the houses. But he has a slanted door that goes into his cellar and it's a lot of fun to slide down the door, then climb up it and slide down again. While we slide, we sing:

Come all you playmates,

Come out and play with me,
And bring your dollies three.
Climb up my apple tree.
Cry down my rain barrel,
Slide down my cellar door,
And we'll be jolly friends forever more.

I'm sorry playmates, I cannot play with you.
My dolly's got the flu. Boo hoo hoo hoo hoo.
Ain't got no rain barrel, ain't got no cellar door,
But we'll be jolly friends forever more.

While we're playing, we try not to make noise but sometimes Mr. Malone comes outside and yells at us kids to be quiet because he has to sleep. Mama keeps telling us to be 'considerate'—that's one of her favourite words—but it's hard to be quiet when you're having fun.

Sometimes we play in our backyard too, if you want to call something the size of Papa's handkerchief a 'yard'. I like to play hide and seek with Michael and the other kids. It's like a jungle back there, and it's fun to run in and out of the peony bushes. The flowers are all kinds of lush colours in June—pinks, whites, reds—and they have the deep smell of earth.

This year, Papa dug a little vegetable garden and planted some cucumbers and radishes and carrots.

I like to eat fresh things from our own garden. Papa jokes, "Since I couldn't go to Israel, I'll be a pioneer in Canada." I laugh, imagining Papa wearing a cowboy hat and a blue suit at the same time.

Mama gets mad when we come into the house with ants from the peonies in our hair and in our clothes. She says, "You kids! Take a bath right now! I don't want the ants crawling all over the house!"

The dead ants look like caraway seeds floating in the bath water. Michael puts them in his bath boats. "Kaboom! You're dead!"

I like to see the ants get sucked down the drain after the bath. We usually take a bath once a week, or when there's an ant emergency.

Nowadays, the street is beginning to fill up with cars that park on the street all night and during the daytime too. Once in a while, a man comes with a horse and wagon. He calls out "Rags! Rags!" as we kids run after his junk wagon and try to peek inside. Or, sometimes a policeman on his horse will go riding through our neighbourhood. Mostly you see cars now, but you still have to be careful not to step into horse 'pies'.

7

Chapter Two

Before Mama made me stop going, she kept saying, "Sarah, you're eight years old. You shouldn't be going to Evelyn's grocery store. You should help me around the house or do your homework instead of wasting your time in an old, musty store."

But I didn't listen to Mama. I thought it was a lot more interesting to visit Evelyn than to dry dishes or do math problems. I especially liked playing on the Ouija board with Evelyn. She said it could look into the future. It turned out she was right.

When we first moved here, Evelyn ran the store with her mother, Mrs. Wise. Her mother called her Evelyn. So did everyone else. A couple of years ago, when her mother died, Evelyn took over the store. And people kept calling her Evelyn.

The store's a great place. There's a rack in front of the store where a customer can get a *Toronto Star* or *Telegram*.

Under the front display window are boxes of candy that Evelyn sells by the penny—licorice, jujubes, gumdrops, jawbreakers, Scotch mints, toffee, and gum. Lately, she's begun selling some candies especially for Halloween—candy kisses, jelly beans, peanuts, and those disgusting toffees that you can get only at this time of year. Good thing, too.

The shelves behind the counter are filled with all kinds of boxes, like Kraft Dinner or Cheerios. I like arranging the cans of Campbell's Tomato Soup or Clover Leaf Salmon or Aylmer Beans so they look neat for the customers. Evelyn lets me stand on her stepladder and I pretend I'm the lookout on a pirate ship—only my treasure isn't gold and jewels, but cans of string beans and bags of flour! Evelyn sells all kinds of cigarettes, like Players, Export A, and Viceroy and even some medicine like Geritol, for 'tired blood' and Aspirin for 'fast headache relief'. On the bottom shelves are cleaning products like Surf Laundry Detergent or SOS Soap Pads.

Near the middle of the store is a rack filled with bread—Toastmaster's white or wholewheat bread or those chocolate cupcakes that are my favourite—the ones with the cream in the middle and the chocolate icing with a white icing swirl on top.

Near the back, there are wooden barrels with sour pickles or olives or herring that you scoop out and put into a container. Evelyn weighs that stuff on her white scale and charges the customer by the pound.

On the side wall, there is an old cooler where Evelyn keeps the cold cuts like ham, tongue, bologna, and hot dogs. There's another cooler beside it with milk and juice and soft drinks.

Sometimes, while we worked in the store together, Evelyn complained, "There's too much competition from the big supermarkets opening up in the neighbourhood. Like Dominion and the A&P. I don't know if I'll be able to stay in business."

I told her, "Don't worry. Sure, some people like to shop at Dominion, but a lot of people still come here."

"Why's that?" she asked. We'd been through that a million times, but she still wanted to hear my answers.

"Well, you're always here."

"That's for sure! Even when I'm sick, I drag myself out of bed to open the store."

"...And you always say 'hello' to everyone who comes into the store."

"Yeah...," Evelyn said.

"And you give better service than the supermarket too."

"What do you mean?"

"You get things off the shelves and put them in bags for the customers," I told her. "But the most important thing is..."

"What?" Now Evelyn was curious.

"You have the best pickles in the neighbourhood!"

Then she joked, "Well, for that last compliment, I'll hold on to the store for a while longer." One time, I heard her say under her breath, "After all, what else do I have?"

"You know, Evelyn, I like it here."

"That's good. Have a pickle."

Another thing I liked about the store was Evelyn's cat, Ginger. He is a big orange and white cat with a splotchy brown spot on his nose. Ginger is the king of the cats. When he goes out at night, he gets into fights with other cats in the neighbourhood. In the morning, he comes slinking back full of scratches and bruises. He spends the day licking his fur from his ears to the tips of his paws, but soon looks for a chance to sneak away again. Evelyn tries to keep Ginger in the apartment behind the store, but Ginger always manages to escape through a door or a window or some opening somewhere. Evelyn can never figure out how he does it.

It was hard to make friends with Ginger. At first, he wouldn't even let me pet him or come close to him. One day, I asked Evelyn if I could feed Ginger and she let me. After that, whenever I had the chance, I would open the can of cat food and put the food in his food dish. Ginger would eat the food, all the while purring like an idling car engine. The advantage about being a grocery store cat is that you get to eat good food. Nothing but Puss 'n Boots cat food—'made from fresh whole fish'—for Ginger!

When I first started going to the store, I just hung around, talking to Evelyn and keeping her company. She seemed to like having me there; I don't know why. Maybe it was because she doesn't have a husband or kids of her own, just Ginger. The other kids say, "Evelyn's a real oddball!" But I don't care what they say. I still like to visit her.

Evelyn is Mama's age, around forty, I think. She always wears a pair of house slippers and a faded cotton dress with a cardigan on top. Her hair is blond-gray and she has small brown eyes in a round face. In fact, her body is round all over. She jiggles when she walks, making her look like a big, cozy pillow. Evelyn knows lots of stories about the neighbourhood. She's lived here her whole life. She tells me about the customers. Mrs. Granger buys all her groceries on credit and complains when she has to pay her bill. Mr. Richard accuses Evelyn of cheating on the bill every time he buys his pack of Players. Mrs. Morley always tries to put something in her pocket that she didn't pay for. Sometimes Evelyn says something; other times she lets it go. It was fun to listen to Evelyn talk. Once in a while, she gave me a free Coke or a stick of black licorice or a jawbreaker. That was when we were still getting along.

Sometimes, Evelyn let me take care of the store for a few minutes while she did something in the

back. She had to make dinner or get a delivery ready or unpack some boxes or even lie down for awhile if she had a headache. I stood behind the high counter that reached almost to my shoulder and I pretended I owned the store and could have anything I wanted.

If a customer came in for a Coke or a pack of cigarettes, I rang the sale up on the cash register and gave the customer the change. There were these buttons, one for each amount of cash, like $1 or 25¢ or 10¢ or 5¢ and I had to push them down hard. Then I pushed the button that said "Cash" and a drawer at the bottom would pop out. There were these little drawers inside, one for each bill of $10 or $5 or $2 or $1, and a big drawer for change. I gave the customer the change and then I closed the drawer with a hard push. I liked the ringing sound the drawer made when it closed. I liked learning the prices of things and felt kind of grown-up being in charge.

14

Chapter Three

My favourite time was when things were slow in the store and Evelyn was in a good mood. Then the lines in her face would smooth out and her usually dull brown eyes would sparkle. She would bring out the Ouija board from its special place in the cupboard. I would sit across from her at the table in the back room of the store.

I remember the first time Evelyn showed me the Ouija board. It was wrapped in a blue velvet cloth. Evelyn carried it carefully, just like Papa handles the velvet bag where he keeps his prayer shawl.

"Sarah, I want to show you something very special," she said, as she stroked the soft material.

"What?"

"You'll see. But you have to promise me something."

"What?" I was getting really curious now.

"That you won't laugh or act silly."

"About what?"

"You'll see. But first, promise," Evelyn insisted. She was acting so serious that she was starting to scare me.

"First, promise," Evelyn insisted.

"OK, I promise," I said.

"Good. Now look," she said, as she unwrapped

the velvet cloth. Inside was a piece of polished wood. Nothing special.

"This is a Ouija board," Evelyn said.

"A what?" I didn't even know if 'Ouija' was English!

"A Ouija board. It's spelled O-U-I-J-A but you say 'Wee-gee'. It can predict the future."

"Like the fortune teller at the Ex?"

"Sort of. But you use this board instead of cards or your palm or tea leaves."

"Oh, I see," I said. But I didn't. This sounded very strange.

"Do you want to try it, Sarah?" she asked.

"Sure," I said. But I wasn't so sure.

Evelyn cleared the dishes off the kitchen table, wiped it with a dishrag, and dried it with a tea towel. She acted like a magician preparing for a show. Then she placed the Ouija board on the table.

A Ouija board is made of hardboard that's smooth and shiny on top. It's harder than the boards in Snakes and Ladders or Parcheesi that we play sometimes. The Ouija board has the capital letters of the alphabet in a curve in the middle—A to M in one line and N to Z underneath. On the bottom of the board are the numbers one to zero and beneath that is the word 'GOOD-BYE'. The word 'YES' is on the top left-hand corner and the word 'NO' is on the top right-hand corner.

Evelyn wiped the board with a silk handkerchief before she used it. She said, "The board must be kept clean and dry."

"Why?" I asked.

"To increase its power." This was sounding stranger by the minute. "Put your fingers on the little board on top. It's called a planchette." I did what she said. "Go ahead. Ask a question."

"What should I ask?"

"Anything you want," she said.

I said the first thing that came into my head. "Will I be rich?" Nothing happened. I was just about to take my fingers off the planchette when I felt my fingers tingling and the planchette started moving slowly, ever so slowly, until it came to the 'YES' position.

"Did you see that?" I whispered.

"Yeah," Evelyn said.

"What does it mean?"

"It must mean that you'll come into some money."

"When?"

"Who knows? The Ouija board is a mystery," she said.

A customer came into the store and I got up to serve her while Evelyn put the Ouija board away. I felt foolish because I had asked such a silly question. I tried to put it out of my mind.

The next day, I was walking home from school and I was pushing some leaves with a stick that I had found. The leaves were on the side of the road and I liked to push them along as I walked. As I was slapping and turning the leaves over, I saw something shiny. It was a silver dollar! I picked it up and held it tightly in my hand until I got home. I put it into my treasure box—a small box Papa gave me that used to have zippers in it—that I keep in my dresser drawer. I didn't tell anyone about it, not even Michael. How could I explain what had happened? He'd only laugh at me.

That was the first time I knew that the Ouija board could predict the future. It wasn't until later that I got more proof than I ever wanted.

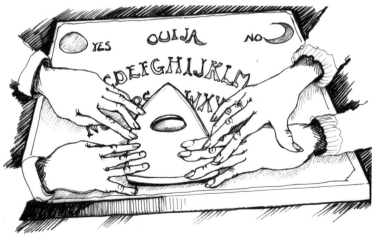

Chapter Four

I need to tell you more about my brother, Michael. He's a skinny kid and small for his age. He's got curly dark brown hair and dark brown eyes. People say that we look more like brother and sister than twins, because I've got light brown hair and hazel eyes.

Michael is always moving around, like Speedy Gonzales in the Bugs Bunny cartoon. He's always making jokes in class and getting into trouble with his teachers. He told me the joke he told John while Miss Insley was writing on the blackboard.

"Knock, knock," said Michael.

"Who's there?" answered John.

"Butter."

"Butter who?"

"I butter not tell you."

Miss Insley made Michael write "I will not talk in class" one hundred times—neatly. That was torture for Michael, because his writing is a scrawl. Miss Insley says maybe he'll be a doctor when he grows up.

Because Michael is so small, the bigger boys used to beat him up, especially when he was walking home from school. The worst one was Lorne, a Canadian kid who lives down the block. As I was walking home with Myra one day, I saw what happened.

A bunch of boys were following Michael, and were getting closer and closer. They kept calling him names like 'Shrimp' and 'Shorty'.

As they got closer, Michael tried to joke his way out of trouble.

"Hey guys," he said, "When's a door not a door?" They kept getting closer.

"When it's ajar. Get it?"

"Yeah, we get it," Lorne said. "And we're gonna get you, too." They surrounded Michael so he couldn't push his way out. Then Lorne jumped on Michael's back and made him gallop around, as if Michael were the horse and Lorne the rider. He was beating Michael on the shoulders with a stick and making him go round and round in a circle.

"Ride 'em, cowboy!" Lorne shouted.

"Dirty Jew! At least he's good for something!" another boy shouted.

"Yeah, give him what he deserves!" shouted a third boy.

Myra ran away. I wanted to help Michael but I was scared of those tough boys. Michael cried, "Get off of me!" but he was too small and there were too many of them.

"Look at the Jew boy. Baby's gonna cry!"

I couldn't stand it anymore. I got so mad I stopped being scared. I ran up to the boys and started beating on Lorne's back with my schoolbag, swinging it around like the Queen of Hearts in Alice in Wonderland who played polo with a flamingo.

"Leave Michael alone!" I screamed. I hit Lorne again and again. He looked behind him, astonished. I kept hitting him until he loosened his grip on Michael and finally slid off his back.

Michael grabbed my hand and yelled, "Come on! Let's get out of here!" We ran away while Lorne called after us, "Chicken! You get a girl to fight your battles! Wait till we get you tomorrow!"

We kept running until we got home. I was breathing so hard it took a few minutes to catch my breath. Michael was mad at me for the rest of the day. He wouldn't talk to me or even look at me.

Finally, when we were getting ready for bed, he said, "What's the difference between a big black cloud and a lion with a toothache?"

"One pours with rain and the other..."

"...roars with pain," I finished.

"Hey, Sarah, thanks," Michael said.

"For what?"

"For helping me today."

"It's okay. That's what big sisters are for."

"Yeah, right. You're a whole half hour older than me."

"Well, every minute counts in this world. So,

show respect, kid."

"Salami, salami, baloney," he said, making a fake bow.

"Good night, little brother," I said.

"Good night, big sister," Michael answered.

The next day, this other big boy, John, decided to be Michael's 'protector'. I don't know why. Maybe it made him feel good to take care of someone else. Anyway, John has the reputation in the neighbourhood for being tough. Since then, none of Lorne's gang bother Michael anymore. No one wants to take the chance of getting into trouble with John.

Another reason that Lorne leaves Michael alone now is that John has been teaching Michael how to wrestle—real wrestling with arm locks and body grabs. Sometimes, John and Michael practise in John's front yard. I can tell that Michael is getting stronger. He walks differently, as if he's got more confidence.

Of course, they never practise when Mama might see. She says, "We suffered enough from people persecuting us during the war. I don't want my son turning into a hoodlum." Mama doesn't understand some things.

But Papa says, "Maybe more Jews would have survived if we'd known better how to defend ourselves, if we'd known how to fight." Mama and Papa started to argue. I hate when they argue because it makes me feel scared. We're all the family we have, and I want everyone to get along. So when they argue, I usually go to the front room and read a book or go outside to play ball—anything to block out the sound of their angry voices.

If Mama knew, she would get mad that John and Michael play by the railroad tracks. She acts kind of crazy if she thinks we're in any kind of danger. She screams and cries and paces back and forth. She's like a mother grizzly protecting her cubs. Maybe she acts that way because she lost her whole family in the war.

Our house isn't far from the tracks. All you have to do is walk the two blocks to Dupont Street, cross the street, and walk through the parking lot of Weston's Bakery. You can smell the yeast from the baking from far away. I get hungry just imagining the thousands and thousands of bread and rolls and buns cooling on the wire racks in the bakery.

We always have enough to eat at home, but nothing extra. When we have unexpected guests, Mama gets really upset.

Papa says, "Just put more water in the soup."

But Mama says, "It doesn't taste the same." I think she always remembers when she and Papa were starving during the war.

After you pass Weston's, you climb up the slope and there are the tracks.

I was always nervous when Michael was playing at the tracks, even though I wouldn't tell Mama. Our school once showed a movie about how dangerous it was to play near the trains. They showed how powerful the trains were, how an accident can happen in a split-second. We even saw kids who had lost an arm or a leg. I had to close my eyes at that part because it was too gruesome to watch. I told Michael to stop playing on the tracks but he wouldn't listen to me.

Chapter Five

It is early autumn. The maple and oak trees in our neighbourhood change from their deep summer green dresses to bright yellows and oranges and reds, as if they are dressing up for a party. The air is crisp and in the morning, a thin layer of frost lies on the windows of the houses and the cars parked on the street. I like to write 'SARAH' and make pictures on the frosty windows. In the evening, you can smell the smoky fires of burning leaves and the coal smoke from the chimneys.

Evelyn has piled pumpkins in front of the store —large and small, skinny and fat. My favourite one is the fattest and roundest one. I want to buy it for Halloween but don't have any money. I can already imagine what face I would carve: upside-down triangles for eyes, a rectangle for a nose, and a big frown with chunky teeth. I'd put a candle inside and it would scare everyone on the block.

I'm getting used to my Grade Three teacher, Miss Johnson, and to the other kids in my class. Miss Johnson is tall and thin and parts her frizzy hair in the middle. She attaches the sides with barrettes and her hair curls up on the ends like a little girl's. She has a clear, soprano voice and leads us in the choir. She stands in front of the classroom, a little stick in her hand, beating out the time. We sing songs like:

Flow gently, sweet Afton
Among thy green braes.
Flow gently, I'll sing thee
A song in thy praise.

I don't know what 'braes' are, but I like the sound of the word anyway. Another song I like is "The Blue Bells of Scotland".

Oh where, tell me where is your
highland laddie gone?
Oh where, tell me where is your
highland laddie gone?
He's gone with streaming banners
where noble deeds are done.
And it's oh! in my heart I wish him safe at home.

That song almost makes me cry when we sing it because it is so sad and high-sounding. Sometimes, I think it's strange to be singing about England and Scotland and its wars hundreds of years ago when my family barely survived World War II.

When I tell Papa about the songs we sing at school, he says, "Listen, Sarah, listen to my songs too." Then he sings to me the song of the fighters in the ghetto:

Zog nit kane mol as du geyst dem letstn veg,

Vile himlen blyeneh farshteln bloiyeh teg.
Kumen vet noch undzer oisgebenkte shoh,
Es vet ah poik tohn undzer trot-mir zainen do!

[Never say this is the final road for you,
Though leadened skies may cover over
                    days of blue,
As the hour that we longed for is so near,
Our step beats out the message--we are here!]

I don't mind being Jewish if I can feel like a Canadian too. Sometimes it's hard to do both.

We have been doing all kinds of activities in the class for Halloween. We cut out shapes of black witches on broomsticks and jack-o'-lanterns and tape them on the windows of the classroom. You can see them from the street whenever you are walking past Palmerston Avenue School.

All the kids in the neighbourhood are talking about the costumes they are planning to wear for Halloween. Michael found the free mask that comes in the Kellogg's Rice Krispies box. He wants to be a cowboy like Roy Rogers. I'm planning to be a witch just like last year. Mama makes me a long nose out of cardboard that she sticks on my own nose with flour paste glue, and I have a long black dress that Mama shortened from one of her old dresses. I am going to carry an old broom and wear black shoes and socks.

28

I like the time when Miss Johnson tells us Halloween stories. She turns off the lights, pulls down the blinds, and lights a candle that flickers on her face. We sit at our desks while she tells us terrifying stories like "The Big Toe" or "The Legend of Sleepy Hollow". Her stories give me a tingling feeling up and down my spine. After that, she turns the lights back on, raises the blinds, blows out her candle, and we do regular schoolwork, like memorizing multiplication tables or doing math problems or drawing maps of Canada and the world.

I go home and tell Mama the stories that Miss Johnson tells us. Mama says, "Those are good stories, but you don't believe they're true, do you?"

"No, I don't," I answer, but secretly, deep down, I think maybe they are.

I hate when Mama is always so practical. I wish she had some imagination. She says in her sad voice, "I don't need any imagination. Life is hard enough without my imagining it's any worse."

"So, imagine it's better," I say.

"I can't," she answers.

I wish Mama wouldn't be so sceptical. After all, she believes in all kinds of superstitions. Some are the same ones that Canadians have. She is always telling us not to walk under a ladder; not to let a black cat cross your path; that breaking a mirror causes seven years of bad luck.

Mama doesn't stop there, for she has a lot of superstitions that she brought from Poland. For example, we aren't supposed to say things are going well—that might tempt the 'Evil Eye' and give us bad luck. Or if, by chance, someone says something bad is going to happen, he has to spit three times over his left shoulder.

Papa has his superstitions too. When he cuts the first slice off a new loaf of bread, he always takes a little nick from the end. You aren't allowed to eat that bit or you'll get bad luck. He thinks that Tuesdays and Thursdays are lucky days to travel; Fridays and Saturdays are not. I think that's because you're not allowed to travel on Shabbat, but I'm not sure.

The strange thing is that when I ask Mama if she believes in the Ouija board, Mama scoffs, "It's just superstitious nonsense." What I would like to know is why a person can believe in some superstitions and not in others. Can the Ouija board really predict the truth or is it just a game? I'm not sure, but I look at my lucky silver dollar every now and again to remind myself that some things can't be explained.

Chapter Six

The week of October 11th began like any other week. I went to school, did my homework, helped Mama around the house. Mama says, "There's always a mess with you kids running around and no place to put things away."

There is only one closet and one dresser for everyone to share, and we have to squeeze all our clothes into them. Not that I have a lot of clothes—two navy blue skirts, three blouses, a sweater, and a pair of warm pants to wear under my skirt when the weather gets cold. I wish that we could wear pants to school and not bother with skirts, but we're not allowed to. Mama washes and mends the clothes a lot to make them last longer. Sometimes, I wish they would disappear so I could get something new for a change.

Because the weather is still warm and the streets are clear of snow, the kids in the neighbourhood often play outside after supper. If there are a lot of us, we play games like 'Red Rover' or 'Hide and Seek' or 'Dodge Ball'. Or we girls like to skip rope:

Girl Guide, Girl Guide, dressed in blue,
These are the motions you must do:
Stand at attention; stand at ease.
Bend your elbows; bend your knees.

Salute to the captain; bow to the queen;
Turn your back on the dirty submarine.
I can do the heel-toe; I can do the splits.
I can do the wiggle-waggle just like this!

If I'm playing by myself or with just one other kid, then we sometimes bounce a ball against the side of the house:

One, two, three, alary,
My first name is Mary.
If you think it necessary,
Look it up in the dictionary.

Mr. Malone hates the noise and is always yelling at us to be quiet. We play together on the street until it gets dark. Then our mothers start calling us to come inside.

"Myra!"

"John!"

"Sarah! Michael!"

That's the end of the games for that day. If the weather is bad, I go over to Myra's house and we play Parcheesi or Snakes and Ladders. I like all those games, but I still tried to visit Evelyn as often as I could.

It was on Wednesday of that week, October 13 to be exact, that was almost the last time I visited Evelyn. Some people say thirteen is an unlucky number. I don't know if that's true or if it's just another superstition. I only know what happened that night.

I went to visit Evelyn after supper, around 6:30. She was sitting behind the counter, and waiting for closing time. The lights were already on, for the days were getting shorter. There were a few people coming in for last-minute shopping—a loaf of bread, a quart of milk, a dozen eggs. I helped her to serve the customers during that last half hour and at 7:00 she locked the door.

"What do you want to do, Sarah?" she asked.

"I don't know," I said, too shy to ask about the Ouija board again.

"Do you want to play with the Ouija board?" she asked, as if reading my mind.

"Sure," I answered.

She took the Ouija board from the shelf. She carefully unwrapped it from its velvet cover, and dusted the board and planchette with the blue silk handkerchief. She concentrated on getting the handkerchief into every tiny corner. I thought it strange that she was kind of sloppy with things in the store but so careful with the Ouija board. At last, she said, "All right. It's ready."

It was quiet in the kitchen behind the store, quieter than at home. Ginger was sleeping in his basket in a warm corner near the stove. Once in a while, he would stretch, purr, and go back to sleep. A dripping faucet from the tap in the bathroom was making a steady monotonous beat, like Miss Johnson's metronome. The wind was moaning and blowing outside, making a loose windowpane rattle.

We put our fingertips on the planchette and closed our eyes. Evelyn said, "You have to empty your mind of everything, of all your thoughts and worries." I tried not to worry about Mama and Papa, how we didn't have enough money, how Michael might get hurt playing by the railway tracks or get beaten up by the boys again.

Evelyn said, "We must open our minds so the Ouija board will answer our questions."

We were quiet for a few minutes. The dripping faucet was getting louder and louder.

Evelyn asked the first question. "Will the store make good business?" Silence. The planchette moved slowly to the 'YES' position. Evelyn sighed, as if she had been holding her breath.

It reminded me of the wicked queen in *Snow White*. She asks the mirror, "Mirror, mirror, on the wall/Who is fairest of us all?" When the mirror answers, "Queen, thou art the fairest of us all!", she relaxes until the next time when she asks the same question. Not that Evelyn was wicked. I almost giggled when I thought of Evelyn poisoning the apples in the store.

Evelyn looked at me and said, "Sarah, it's your turn."

I didn't know what to say. There were so many questions spinning around in my head. I was thinking of Halloween and going trick or treating. The question "Will the weather be good?" suddenly came popping out of my mouth. I didn't even know I'd been thinking about the weather. But there was the question, hanging in the air like a guillotine about to drop.

I opened my eyes and stared at the board. The planchette was still for a moment, and then started to move around, back and forth, back and forth, from the centre of the board to the 'NO' corner. Back and forth, as if it had a mind of its own, not stopping, not hesitating. I wanted to take my fingers off the planchette but couldn't. They seemed stuck onto it, as if by a magic spell. The 'NO' echoed in my head and seemed to bounce around like a crazy ping pong ball, repeating its refrain over and over, as if my head were hollow. Ginger got up from his bed and arched his back.

The planchette wouldn't stop moving until Evelyn demanded, "When? When?" Slowly, the planchette spelled out the letters F-R-I-D-A-Y. Ginger walked to my chair and started to rub against my legs. The fur on his back was stiff and his eyes were glowing yellow orbs.

"Friday the what?" I whispered. The planchette moved to the numbers 1 and 5. Ginger began to meow.

Evelyn looked at me. She tried to smile reassuringly but her eyes were worried. She asked, "Will people get hurt?"

The planchette raced to the 'YES' on the board.

I had had enough. "I want to stop," I said.

"Only one more question," Evelyn said. "I want to know something." I shook my head but Evelyn continued anyway. "Will people die?" she asked.

'YES' was the answer. Ginger's fur was standing up and his tail was stiff.

I yelled, "Stop! I'm getting scared!" I took my fingers off the planchette. They felt hot, as if they'd just been sitting on a bed of coals.

Evelyn said, "You're right. Me too." She put her fingers on the planchette and moved it to GOOD-BYE.

We sat there, not saying a word, the Ouija board sitting between us. It was silent. Still. I heard the dripping of the tap and the wind blowing through the trees. I picked Ginger up and put him in my lap. As I stroked his soft fur, he quieted down and began to purr.

Evelyn wrapped the Ouija board in its velvet cloth and placed it back on the shelf. Her hands were shaking and there were lines on her forehead I'd never noticed before. She poured water into the kettle and placed it on the stove. "I need a nice cup of tea," she said.

"Do you think it could be true?" I asked.

"What?" Evelyn seemed to be daydreaming, just like Michael sometimes does.

"Is it true? What the Ouija board said? About people dying?"

"I don't think so. The weather doesn't get that bad in Toronto. I know there were some big fires and flu epidemics a long time ago, but that doesn't happen now. People don't die of the weather in Toronto, for Pete's sake!"

It sounded like she was trying to reassure herself as much as me. It wasn't working.

"But I read in *The Wizard of Oz* about Dorothy and her dog, Toto. They got picked up by a tornado and landed in Oz." I paused. "Evelyn, does Toronto get tornadoes?"

"Of course not. That's just a story."

"Are you sure?"

"Positive. And even if it were going to happen, the weather office would warn us on the radio. Don't you think?" The kettle was making a whistling sound. It was comforting somehow. Evelyn put a tea bag in the brown teapot and poured boiling water into the pot. She covered the pot with a flowered tea cozy.

"I guess so."

"So, stop worrying, Sarah."

"All right. I'll try."

"Good." She poured the tea into a cup and sipped it slowly. She seemed to forget about me for a minute. Looking up, she asked, "How about a piece of licorice on your way out?" I could take a hint.

"Thanks," I said. I stood up and Ginger jumped off my lap. He went to his food dish while I took a piece of black licorice and left the store. "Bye, Evelyn," I said.

There was no answer. The door squeaked as I shut it behind me. I looked back through the lit window and saw Evelyn sitting at the table. She had pulled her cardigan tightly around her chest, and her hands were cradling the teacup, as if she were trying to get warm.

Chapter Seven

The next morning at breakfast, I started to tell Mama about what had happened. I was trying to eat my Cream of Wheat. It is full of lumps that make me gag when I try to swallow. But Mama makes me eat whatever she spoons into my bowl. I think it's disgusting, but Mama always says, "It's a sin to waste food." I think there are too many sins, but I don't have the nerve to tell that to Mama.

She continues, "Besides, it says on the box that Cream of Wheat has lots of iron." What does that mean, anyway? Are there little pieces of iron in the cereal? Thinking about the iron doesn't make it easier to swallow. I wish we had a cat. I'd give him my Cream of Wheat. Poor cat!

"Mama, last night I played on the Ouija board with Evelyn…," I said.

Mama interrupted, "That Ouija board again? I told you, Sarah, I don't like you to play that game. It's just superstition and a waste of time."

"But Mama, it said ..."

"No, I don't want to hear about it. Now eat your cereal. You have to go to school in five minutes. I don't want you to be late."

"But Mama..."

"No," she said. "Eat!"

I choked down my cereal and got ready for school. There's no use arguing with Mama when she makes up her mind about something.

All morning, I couldn't concentrate in class. I kept thinking about what the Ouija board had said, and I didn't know what to do or whom to talk to.

During recess, we girls were playing 'Yoki', the game where you tie elastics together to make two springy cords. You hop on one foot while you hook your other foot over the elastic. We sing this song:

> *Yoki and the Kaiser,*
> *Yoki addy ay,*
> *Tam-ba so-ba,*
> *Sa-du, sa-day.*

My foot kept getting tangled in the elastics until I finally gave up. I left the game and started to walk around the schoolyard. Myra ran after me. "What's the matter, Sarah?" she asked.

"Nothing." I wasn't sure if I could trust her, especially after she'd run away the other day.

"Well, it must be something. You look like Superman when he got exposed to a chunk of Kryptonite."

I decided I had to talk to someone. "Myra, if I tell you something, will you promise not to laugh?"

"I wouldn't laugh. We're best friends, aren't we?"

"Yeah." I decided we were. "But will you promise?"

"Okay, if it'll make you feel better."

"Cross your heart and hope to die?"

"Cross my heart and hope to die," she said.

"Okay, I'll tell you." I took a big breath. "Yesterday, I went to Evelyn's store and we played with her Ouija board."

"So? What's so funny about that?"

"It's not funny, like ha, ha funny. The Ouija board said something really scary."

"Like what?"

I blurted it out. "It said the weather's going to be really bad on Friday the 15th. Some people will get hurt."

"You're kidding!"

"No, I'm not. It even said some people will die! Myra, I'm really scared."

"Well…do you think it'll really happen?"

"Who knows?"

"Should we do something about it?"

"Like what?"

"Tell Miss Johnson. She's nice. Maybe she'll have an idea."

"I don't want to, Myra. I'd feel stupid to ask her."

"Me too. What else can we do?"

"I don't know. Maybe nothing. Maybe something. Oh, I wish I was a grown-up. Then I'd know what to do!"

"Is there someone else you can talk to?"

"Maybe my dad?"

"Yeah. Good idea. Listen. I just thought of some-thing. Are you sure it's this Friday the 15th? Maybe it's another one, like years and years from now?"

"Maybe..."

"Listen, let's just forget about it for now. Let's go play Yoki. Okay?"

"Okay."

We played until the bell rang. I tried to forget about my worries until school was over.

Chapter Eight

While we were eating supper—meatloaf, mashed potatoes, and canned peas—I kept thinking about the Ouija board.

"Hey, Sarah, why are you so quiet?" asked Michael, kicking me under the table.

"None of your business," I said, kicking him back. I knew he would laugh at me if he knew.

"What key is hardest to turn?"

I thought for a minute. "A donkey!" I kicked him.

"What did one wall say to the other?"

"I don't know. What?"

"I'll meet you at the corner!" He kicked me back.

Mama said, "Sarah, after supper, I want you to help me with the dishes."

"But Mama," I said, "I'm always helping with the housework and Michael doesn't have to. It's not fair!"

"Listen to your mother," Papa said. "Michael helps too. He works in the yard and shovels the snow in the winter." Michael stuck his tongue out at me.

"Michael…" Papa warned. Papa always expects us to be polite.

"Okay, Papa. Here's one for you. Where was Moses when the lights went out?"

"What lights?" Papa asked. "There were lights in Egypt?" Papa doesn't get our jokes.

"I know!" I said. "In the dark!"

"No, stupid! Under the bed, looking for matches!" I almost kicked Michael again.

After supper was over, I helped dry the dishes while we listened to some music on CJBC. Then I went to talk to Papa.

The stairs going down to the cellar are steep and covered with old linoleum. There's a cracked cement floor and an old coal furnace in the corner that heats up the house. Next to the furnace is a pile of dusty coal that makes me sneeze when I go near. There are two washtubs and an old wringer washing machine on the other side of the cellar, in another corner.

Mama is always talking about getting a new washing machine. She showed me a new McClary machine from the Eaton's catalogue that costs $129.95. "Maybe I'll wait until it goes on sale," Mama always says. I like pushing the clothes through the wringers and watching how the water drips into the washtub on one side and how the clothes come out on the other side, all damp and flattened out like a soggy pancake.

My favourite place in the cellar is near Papa's sewing machine. On a big table, he pins the material he's sewing or presses with the heavy iron that I can't even lift. I like the smell of new material, of the steam from the iron, of the dampness of the cellar. Papa hammered some nails into a board and on each nail he placed a different spool of thread. I love all the colours—the greens, purples, reds, blues, even the shiny blacks and greys. It looks like my box of water-colour paints, only better.

Papa sits at his old Singer sewing machine, the lamp shining on his work. While he sews, he sings Yiddish songs or tells me stories about the 'old country'.

Ot azoy nate a shnyder,
Ot azoy varft er shtech.
Ot azoy nate a shnyder,
Ot azoy varft er shtech.
A shnyder nate un nate un nate,
Un hut kaduches nit kine brate.

[This is how a tailor sews.
This is how he makes his stitches.
This is how a tailor sews.
A tailor sews and sews and sews.
He gets a fever but no bread.]

I like to listen to the whirring of the sewing machine and feel the warmth from the lamp. Papa's feet go back and forth on the pedals. The material flows beneath his fingers as if he's a magician with cloth. While Papa is sewing, he forgets his worries

46

about money and his bad memories about the war. Everything is dark except for the circle of light around Papa and me and the sewing machine.

"So, what's bothering you, Sarah? I can always tell when something is wrong." I watch Papa basting the sleeves of a man's suit jacket. In and out of the cloth goes the needle, pushed by Papa's funny thimble on his thumb.

"I went to Evelyn's grocery store last night and…"

"And…?"

"And the Ouija board said that soon the weather is going to get bad. Papa, it said that some people will get hurt, or…even die."

"The Ouija board said that?"

"Yes, Papa."

"So, what do you think?"

"I don't know, Papa. Part of me believes it and feels scared. The other part agrees with Mama."

"What does Mama say?"

"That I shouldn't pay any attention to it."

"Listen, Sarah, if something scares you, it's better to talk about it. Even if you can't do anything about it, it's still better to get it out in the open."

"I guess so. But isn't there something that we can do?"

"Like what, Sarah?"

"Like tell the Mayor," I said.

"Maybe. But I don't think he'd listen to you. Anyway, if there's any real danger, I'm sure the mayor knows about it already. Don't you think so?"

"Yeah, I guess so."

"Listen to me, Sarah. The best thing to do is to forget about all of this. The Ouija board is just a game. Nothing is going to happen to hurt you or anyone else. Do you think you can do that?"

"I'll try, Papa."

"Good," Papa said. Under his breath, he added, "Sometimes a person must act. Sometimes he must try to forget." I stayed in the cellar for a while longer, watching the jacket take shape beneath Papa's nimble fingers. Then I went upstairs to finish my homework. I thought that since there wasn't anything I could do, I might as well stop worrying about it…as if I could.

Chapter Nine

That night, I dreamed that I was standing beside a river. The sky was dark with grey clouds scudding across its surface. The water was rising higher and higher, splashing my feet; the current swirling faster and faster. The water was at my knees, my thighs, my shoulders. Trees, animals, houses, people, were being overtaken by the rushing flood. I was grabbed by the cold arms of the river and was swept along with the current. I couldn't breathe. I was drowning! I woke up with a sour taste in my mouth, my breath coming in short gasps. I went back to sleep again, but I tossed and turned the rest of the night.

It was Friday morning and I was still feeling nauseous when I came into the kitchen. Mama was standing at the sink and washing the dishes. I sat down at the kitchen table. "What's wrong with you?" Michael asked as he sat eating his toast across from me. "You've been acting really weird lately."

I picked up a spoon that felt as heavy as a bulldozer. "I don't know. I just don't feel like going to school," I answered. I stared at the Rice Krispies getting soggy in the bowl.

"Well, that's nothing new for me. I feel like that every morning!"

"Yeah, but I don't. I like school and I like Miss

Johnson." I put my spoon down.

"She's sure nicer than my battle-axe of a teacher!"

"Mama, I feel kind of sick this morning, like I'm going to throw up." I put my head down on my arms. Michael started singing,

Great green gobs of greasy, grimy gopher guts,
Mutilated monkey meat,
Little birdies' dirty feet.
Great green gobs of greasy, grimy gopher guts,
And I forgot my spoon.

"Michael!" Mama said warningly. Michael suddenly seemed very interested in the cereal box.

Mama dried her hands on the dishtowel and walked over to the table. She felt my forehead. "No fever," she said. "You have to go to school."

There's no use arguing with Mama. I carried my bowl to the sink, put on my jacket, and left for school with Michael. He tried to cheer me up with one of his stupid jokes again.

"What goes up when the rain comes down?"

"I know that one," I said. "An umbrella." The fresh air was making me feel better.

We started to play our game with the cars. We try to guess what kind of car we're coming to before we get too close. Michael always wins because he knows the models of cars inside and out. He'll say, "There's a '53 Oldsmobile 88" or "Look at that nifty '51 Buick Deluxe sedan" or "Wow! A '41 Dodge Custom sedan!" He can spot them half a block away.

Before I knew it, we had reached school. We parted at the school yard, Michael to play with his friends and I to play with mine.

Although we're twins, the principal decided to put us into different classes. Mama doesn't like that much—she thinks that twins should stay together—but she doesn't want to argue with the principal, especially since she still has trouble with her English. So, Michael and I usually don't hang around together at school: one, because we play with kids from our own classes, and two, girls play with girls and boys play with boys.

The morning dragged on and nothing that we were doing was interesting. I was tired of learning about the Canadian provinces and practising the multiplication tables. The air was feeling heavy and I was getting a headache.

When we went home for lunch, Mama had prepared my favourite—grilled cheese sandwiches and Campbell's Tomato Soup made with milk. I like being home at lunch time. While we eat, we usually listen to the radio. I especially like the show on CJBC called "Small Types Club". The announcer plays the song,

"Teddy Bears' Picnic" at the beginning of the show and there are stories and songs and games and sometimes a contest that you can enter. When the show is over, we have to "Sco-o-t" off to school. Rich kids have television sets, but I still like the radio. I can imagine my own pictures in my head.

All the kids like Friday afternoon. That's when we get to do art and when Miss Johnson teaches us new songs. That afternoon, Miss Johnson played some music on the record player called "Night on Bald Mountain" by a composer called Mussorgsky, she told us. The music was really scary and we were supposed to draw a picture on black paper with our crayons that had to do with Halloween. I worked on mine for a while and almost forgot about the Ouija board.

Miss Johnson stood beside my desk. "Tell me about your drawing, Sarah," she asked.

"It has a full yellow harvest moon with spooky trees blowing in the wind and a house whose windows look like eyes staring out at the street."

"I like your picture, Sarah. You've really captured the mood of Halloween."

"Thanks, Miss Johnson."

"I'm going to put it up on our bulletin board. Would you like that?"

I just nodded. I felt happy all the way home.

When we walked into the house, I could smell the familiar mixture of floor polish and roasting chicken that always greeted me on Fridays. Not only was it the end of the school week, but that evening was the beginning of Shabbat. I loved the quiet of the house, especially after Mama said the blessing over the candles. I loved the taste of the egg bread, *challah*, and the way everything was clean and shining. I loved the white tablecloth and the delicious chicken soup that Mama made. Our family only goes to synagogue once a year, on the High Holidays, but on Friday night, I always feel more Jewish than at any other time.

Papa must feel like that too. He sometimes asks, "Where was God during the War?"

Mama says, in her stubborn way, "God was there. He was just quiet."

"So quiet he let six million Jews die?"

"So quiet. But God is still here."

"Believe what you want," Papa says, "but I'll believe what I want." Mama just shakes her head.

That night, as we sat at the dinner table, I heard the radio announcer saying, "Weather forecast for this evening, October 15. Rain tonight. Cloudy with occasional showers Saturday. Little change in temperature. Winds north, 40 to 50 miles per hour, this evening, decreasing overnight to northwest 30 miles per hour on Saturday. Low tonight 45, high Saturday 55."

"I'd better make sure that all the windows and doors are closed properly," Papa said. "Sometimes the tenants keep the windows open and the rain comes into the house."

"You're right," Mama replied tiredly. "Will you check them after supper while I do the dishes?"

"Sure." We continued to eat our supper. Mama always makes a special supper on Friday night—fish, chicken soup, roast chicken, and roast potatoes. She baked my favourite cake for dessert—a strudel with cocoa and jam—and she let me have a cup of sweet tea with lemon in it. I was glad my appetite was back.

After supper, I wanted to go over to Evelyn's store. I was putting on my jacket when Mama called, "Where are you going, Sarah?"

"Outside. I want to get some fresh air," I answered. I didn't want to tell Mama that I was going to Evelyn's because I thought she would get mad at me, especially because of what had happened the last time I went there.

"All right, but stay on the verandah. It's starting to rain."

"Okay, Mama."

Michael was getting his jacket on too. "I'm going to John's house," he said.

"Be back soon," Mama called.

"Okay, Mama."

I asked, "Why do I have to stay on the verandah while Michael gets to go to John's?"

She said, "Boys are different. I worry more about you."

"I'm just as tough as Michael."

"I don't care. I said stay on the verandah, you stay on the verandah."

"Mama!"

"Do what I tell you."

I didn't answer Mama. I was too mad. Michael and I both squeezed out the door together. He headed towards John's house while I started to cross the street. "See you later," I said.

"Hey, I thought Mama told you to stay on the verandah," Michael answered.

"I don't care. I'm going to visit Evelyn."

"You're going to get into trouble," Michael warned.

"I'm going anyway."

"Suit yourself."

"Hey, are you really going over to John's house, or are you going to play by the tracks again?"

"None of your business!"

"You'd better not get into trouble either, Michael," I said.

"Don't worry about me. See you later, alligator," he replied.

"After awhile, crocodile."

Chapter Ten

When I reached the grocery store, it was already past seven o'clock. The big ceiling lights in the store were off, and as I peeked through the big, front window, I could see only the dim light from the milk cooler. I walked around to the side and knocked on the door. It was starting to rain and I was glad when Evelyn came to the door. Ginger was meowing at her feet.

"Come in. Come in, Sarah. Don't stand there getting wet," she said. I went in and she quickly closed the door behind me. I took my jacket off and put it on a hook in the hallway. I followed Evelyn to the kitchen. There were a few dirty dishes left in the sink and I could hear the faucet, still dripping in the bathroom. I wondered why she didn't get it fixed. Was she lazy, like Mama said, or couldn't she afford it?

The Ouija board was already set up on the kitchen table. "Did you know I was coming over?" I asked.

"No, but I wanted to ask the Ouija board some questions."

"Why?"

"I don't know. I guess the storm's made me nervous. Anyway, I've been thinking and worrying since the other night when you were here."

"Really?"

"Sure. Did you think that adults don't worry?"

"No, I know they do. I just didn't know that you do."

"Yeah, I do. Probably more than most." I could tell she was feeling uncomfortable talking about it. She finished wiping the board and asked, "Are you ready?"

"I think so."

She squeezed my arm reassuringly. We put our fingers on the planchette and Evelyn asked her usual question, "Will the store make good business?"

'YES' was the answer.

She asked, "What will be in the future?" Ginger was walking back and forth between us and making a low growling sound in his throat.

The planchette started to move to the letter 'H' first, then another 'H'. What did that mean? I wondered. Evelyn asked once more, "What will happen tonight?"

The planchette moved to the letters 'H' and then 'H' again. I knew that sometimes the Ouija board answers questions in short forms like codes, but I didn't have any idea what 'H-H' might mean. Evelyn looked as puzzled as I was.

I asked, "Will anyone get hurt?"

The planchette moved so fast to the 'YES' that I

had trouble keeping my fingers on it.

I didn't want to ask the next question but Evelyn knew what I was thinking. "Will anyone...die?" she asked.

"YES," it answered. "YES." Ginger jumped up on my lap, his back arched, his claws digging into me. It hurt and I took my fingers off the planchette. "I don't want to do this anymore," I said. "I'm getting scared."

She took her fingers off the planchette too. "You're right. Let's stop."

"I want to go home." I stood up and Ginger jumped off my lap. Just then I noticed the howling of the wind and the rain beating hard against the windows. Water was trying to sneak into the store, its fingers poking into the cracks beneath the door and the spaces around the windows. I stood by the door. I was afraid to leave but didn't want to stay.

"Evelyn, I want to go home. Right now!" I yelled.

"Sure, Sarah, don't worry." She gave me a hug, stiffly, like someone not used to giving hugs. When she opened the door, the rain was falling so hard that I couldn't see our house across the street. The rain was a gigantic curtain of water, like Niagara Falls, and lightning was streaking across the sky. The street had turned into a rushing river, with leaves and branches clogging up the gutters. I imagined myself falling, falling, and being carried away by the torrent. It was just like my nightmare, only now it was for real. We had to push the door hard to shut it against the blowing gale.

"Evelyn, I want to go home!" I cried.

"Just a minute. Just a minute." She paced up and down the aisle of the store, the boxes and cans looking eerie in the pale light coming from the back and from the flashes of lightning.

At the sound of one tremendous thunderclap, Ginger screeched and ran under the counter. He hissed and spit, his eyes shining yellow in the dim light.

"What's your telephone number, Sarah?" Evelyn asked.

"MELROSE 4700."

Mama must have answered on the first ring, so quickly did Evelyn say, "Hello." There was a pause. "This is Evelyn, from the corner store. I'm calling to let you know Sarah is here." Another pause. "Listen, it's not my fault she's here. She came by herself." Pause again. "Well, don't blame me!" Evelyn's voice was getting louder. "I'm just phoning to tell you she's here. She needs help getting home." I could hear Mama yelling on the other end. "Yes, all right. I'll keep her here until your husband comes over. Bye." Evelyn slammed the receiver down hard.

"I don't know why your mother is so mad at me,"

she said. "Didn't you tell her you were coming here?"

"Well…no…I didn't want to get into trouble," I said.

Evelyn looked at me accusingly. "Why would you get into trouble?" she demanded.

"Mama said I shouldn't come here."

"Why not?"

" Because…because of the Ouija board."

"The Ouija board?"

"Mama says it's all superstition. That I was getting too upset by the whole thing."

Evelyn's face turned red and she had trouble looking me in the eye. "If your mother doesn't want you to come here anymore, then you shouldn't come," she said in a hurt voice. "I don't want you to get into trouble for visiting me."

There was a knock at the door. Evelyn opened it and Papa was standing there, the rain dripping from his big, black umbrella onto his thin jacket.

"Hello, Evelyn," he said coolly. She nodded her head in his direction, but she was acting strangely, as if she didn't want to be noticed

"Hurry up, Sarah. The storm is terrible outside," he said.

"Okay, Papa. I'm coming," I said, as I zipped up my jacket.

"You scared us all to death. We didn't know

where you were."

"Sorry, Papa." I only had time to say, "Sorry, Evelyn. 'Bye," before Papa grabbed my arm. When Evelyn pushed the door closed against the wind, I could see that her eyes were wet. It must have been the rain falling on her face.

63

Chapter Eleven

Papa and I were struggling across the road. He was trying to hold onto his umbrella with one arm while he had his other arm around me. The wind was pulling the umbrella out of his hand and he was straining to hold onto it. It wasn't much use anyway. Rain was seeping down my neck and up my sleeves and plastering the hair down my face.

Suddenly, there was an enormous streak of lightning that lit up the sky like a giant Roman candle. It struck the trunk of the old maple tree on Mr. Malone's front yard. The tree groaned and cracked and split into a million pieces. Its branches went flying in all directions and a huge one charged us like a shrieking wild animal. The air smelled of water and smoke and fire.

Papa just stood there on the curb, as if he were paralysed. He let go of his umbrella and it was carried off by the wind. I pulled on Papa's arm. "Papa!" He didn't move. I screamed, "Papa! Run!"

Papa shook his head, as if to clear it. He grabbed my arm tightly while I hung onto his coat and we ran across the street as if we were one body, one person. Leaves and twigs were brushing against my face and legs and the cold, wet rain was stinging my eyes. A huge branch landed on the sidewalk where we had been standing just seconds before.

We were both panting and shaking when we finally reached the verandah. Just as Papa opened the door, Mama came rushing out. She grabbed me by the shoulders and gave me a fierce hug. She was suffocating me but it felt good too.

"Sarah! Avram!" she sobbed, "I was watching from the window but everything happened so fast! I thought you'd be killed by that tree! Come inside. Come inside." We hurried into the house and pushed the door closed behind us.

As Mama handed us some dry towels, she asked, "Where's Michael? Have you seen him?"

"No," I said. I was shaking all over and my voice trembled.

"Wasn't he with you?" Papa asked.

"No. He went to John's house. Remember?" I asked. "Isn't he home yet?"

"Do you see him?" Mama snapped. "I'm going to phone John right away." Just then, the doorbell rang. Papa went to open it.

A railway policeman was holding Michael by the arm. Michael's hair was stuck to his face and his clothes were dripping puddles onto Mama's clean floor. For once, Mama didn't seem to mind. She grabbed Michael and gave him a big hug. She seemed to have enough hugs for everyone today.

"I'm Henry Fairweather from the CN Police. Is this your boy?" he asked.

"Sarah, what's he saying?" asked Papa.

"What happened?" asked Mama.

"He's a policeman from the railway," I explained in Yiddish. "He wants to know if Michael's your son."

"Yes!" said Papa.

I explained to the man, "My parents can't speak English very well."

"Oh, I see, but this is your brother, isn't he?" said the man.

"Sure he's my brother!" I said. "He's a brat, too," I added.

"I am not," Michael said. I could see the rain hadn't drowned his tongue.

"Well, tell your parents I found him and his friend playing at the tracks. I thought I'd better bring 'em home. Because of the storm and all…" I explained it all to Mama and Papa. Michael was looking down at the wet floor. For once, he didn't have anything to say.

"Tell the man thank you, Sarah. That we were very worried about Michael," Mama said.

"What did your mother say?" Mr. Fairweather asked.

"That she was worried about my brother," I said.

"Well, tell her he's okay now. But if I ever catch him playin' around the tracks again, I'll charge him with trespassing." I told Mama and Papa what he said. Papa said, "Tell him he won't see Michael at the tracks ever again. I'll make sure." I explained Papa's words to the man.

"All right then. I'll let it go this time. Good night," he said.

"Good night," Papa said.

"Thank you," Mama said. She dragged Michael inside and closed the door. She pointed her finger at him. "Don't even move, Michael! Not one step," she warned. He stood there, wet and shivering until Mama brought him a dry towel too.

We changed into our pajamas and bathrobes and slippers while Papa made cocoa for everyone. We all sat at the kitchen table while Papa poured the steaming cocoa into our cups.

Papa was quiet at first. Then he said, "Michael, you have to promise…"

Michael looked at Papa.

"…that you will never, ever, play by the railway tracks again."

Michael paused for a minute. "Michael…" Papa said.

"All right, Papa, I won't," Michael agreed. "I was really scared this time." He shivered. "I won't go again."

"Good," said Papa.

It was Mama's turn. "As for you, Sarah, you have to promise not to go to Evelyn's store again."

I didn't want to promise. It wasn't fair.

"Sarah…"

"All right, Mama. I promise. But I still like Evelyn."

"You can like her, but you can't go there again."

"Ever," Papa said.

"One more thing," Mama added. "If I ever catch either of you lying again, I'll…I'll…I'll make you scrub the kitchen floor for a month!"

"Even Michael?" I asked.

"Especially Michael!" Papa roared.

"Sorry, Mama," I said. "I won't lie ever again."

"Me neither," said Michael.

"Good. So that's the end of that," Papa said.

"Now finish your cocoa and off to bed with both of you," Mama said. Mama and Papa kissed us good-night and we slunk off to bed. As we left the kitchen, I heard Mama say to Papa, "Twins! Double the trouble!"

Papa answered, a smile in his voice, "Yes, and twice the fun!" I could almost hear Mama shaking her head.

Before we went to sleep, Michael said, "What did the ground say when it began to rain?"

"I don't know. What?"

"If this goes on for long, my name will be…"

"Mud!"

"Goodnight, Sarah."
"Goodnight, Michael."

Chapter Twelve

The next morning, Michael was still sleeping when I came into the kitchen. Mama was peeling potatoes at the kitchen table while she listened to the radio on CFRB. The announcer was saying, "Hurricane Hazel created havoc in Toronto during the night."

I said, "Mama, now I know! I know what the Ouija board was trying to tell us. 'H-H' stands for Hurricane Hazel! I just knew something bad was going to happen!"

"Shh, Sarah, let me listen," Mama said.

The announcer continued, "7.2 inches of rain fell on Metropolitan Toronto in the last 24 hours. The wind reached 55 miles per hour, gusting up to 72 miles per hour. Homes and property were destroyed by the surging waters of the Don and Humber Rivers; lives were snapped up, with hardly a moment's notice. The Humber River rose 20 to 30 feet above its usual level.

"Automobiles were thrown around in the onrushing flood water. Close to Number Seven highway, homes were inundated. Hundreds of trees were ripped out by the roots and were carried away by the flood.

"At least eighty people have been killed, fifteen of them children. Many more people have been injured and thousands have been left homeless.

"This is the worst disaster the city of Toronto has ever known. The estimate of damage at this moment is at least $10,000,000. Stay tuned to CFRB for the latest developments."

The Ouija board had been right after all! "Mama, we could have been killed last night," I cried.

"Come here, Sarah," Mama said. She stood up and put her arms around me. "The hurricane's over now. There's nothing more to worry about. Thank God, our family's safe and we should be grateful. Go get dressed. I'll make some French toast from leftover *challah* and then we'll go shopping."

After breakfast, we read about Hurricane Hazel in *The Star*. There were a lot of photographs of amazing rescues and close calls. There was a story about people who had to leave their cars and climb trees while their cars were swept away in the flood down the Humber and Don Rivers; commuter trains were derailed; highways were blocked; forty bridges were washed away.

The news of the catastrophe went on and on all morning long. I didn't want to hear any more. There were some happy stories, but a lot of sad ones too.

I needed a break. So, Michael and I shared the comics. I like "Little Lulu" and "Little Orphan Annie"; Michael likes "Popeye" and "Terry and the Pirates". It's a good thing we don't fight over the comics.

That afternoon Mama said, "We're going shopping. I want to see what happened in the neighbourhood, and you children need new clothes." We walked with Mama to Honest Ed's.

That's the big store not far from us, the one with the flashing coloured lights all around. It's always fun to go there because there are funny signs on the outside of the store, like 'Often Imitated but Never Duplicated' and photographs of Ed Mirvish, the owner, with famous people like movie stars and politicians.

I always try to keep close to Mama when we're in the store because it's easy to get lost in the crowds of people and the aisles going every which way, like a maze, and three flights of stairs. Mama says things are always cheaper there, but you have to shop carefully. You can't take anything back like at Eaton's or Simpson's.

Mama got Michael two pairs of socks, 99¢ each, and a pair of jeans with cotton plaid lining and cuffs for $3.29. She bought me a hat for $1.49 and a pink sweater, just like Myra's, for $3.99. (I like looking at the prices. I guess it's a habit from when I helped Evelyn in the store.) We waited a long time at the cash register to pay for them, but I didn't mind waiting because everybody was talking about Hurricane Hazel.

The woman in front of us was talking about a

baby girl called Nancy Thorpe. "She's only four months old," the woman said. "The fire chief in Long Branch rescued her. But just when he was going back to save the rest of the family, the house was swept away."

"That's terrible," Mama said.

The woman continued, "I know. Nancy's parents and her two-year-old brother died in the hurricane." It was our turn to pay. Mama counted out the money carefully and we went outside.

There was a man selling popcorn and roasted peanuts and candy apples from his wagon. Mama bought a bag of popcorn for each of us and a bag of peanuts for herself. I love the taste of butter and salt on the warm popcorn and I like to lick my fingers when I'm finished.

We walked home through the broken branches and strewn rubble that lay on the roads and sidewalks of our neighbourhood. Everything had been tossed around by the fierce winds: baby strollers, lawn chairs, garbage cans, loose boards, kids' wagons, tricycles. People were outside, cleaning up the debris and sweeping their walks.

Mama said, "I hope God has a very large broom to clean up all the mess He's made!" She held me by one hand and Michael by the other. The sun felt warm on our faces and there was a gentle breeze blowing through the golden leaves.

Michael said, "Hey, I know a good joke for today."

"What?"

"Knock, knock."

"Who's there?"

"Wayne."

"Wayne who?"

"Wayne, Wayne, go away. Come again another day." We let go of Mama's hands and raced along the sidewalk, pushing and shoving each other all the way home.

The next day, I broke my promise to Mama. I had to talk to Evelyn one last time. I didn't care if I had to wash the floor for a year.

The store was closed, but when I knocked on the side door, Evelyn's pale face peeked out through the space between the curtains.

"Evelyn!" I called. "I have to talk to you!"

She opened the door and let me in. "I was worried about you," she said. "With the hurricane and... everything."

"I'm fine. See?" And I spun around, making my skirt swirl around my legs.

"And you weren't hurt?"

"Not a bit." I heard Evelyn let out her breath, as if she'd been holding it for a long time.

"I'm glad. Real glad," she said.

"Evelyn?"

"Yes?"

"I've got to tell you something."

"What?"

"I…I…can't come here anymore."

"You mean, to help out?"

"No. Ever." My throat was burning. I started to cry. "Mama won't let me."

Evelyn sat down on a chair. "I see."

"Evelyn…"

"Yeah?"

"You've been great. I'll never forget you."

"I won't forget you, either."

"Evelyn?" I said, wiping my eyes with my sleeve.

"Yeah?"

"Can I give you a hug?"

"Sure you can!" We hugged. I think we both felt better.

When I left Evelyn's store, I was munching on a pickle. I looked back and saw Ginger sitting on the window ledge. On his face was a knowing expression.

Well, I've done what Miss Johnson told me to do. I've written down everything I can remember about the day Hurricane Hazel came to town. The city changed a lot after that. So did I.

Historical Note

Hurricane Hazel struck Toronto on October 15, 1954. The facts about the storm as told in this story are all true. It was the worst disaster the city had ever had. Eighteen centimetres of rain fell, dumping 100 billion litres of water on an unprepared city. The Humber and Don Rivers, Highland and Etobicoke Creeks rose, swelled, and burst. Winds whipped through the city at more than 110 kilometres per hour. Hundreds of trees were ripped out by the roots and fell to the flood. Forty bridges were swept away. Property damage amounted to $25,000,000. Hurricane Hazel killed 83 people and left 5,000 people homeless.

After the hurricane, the province of Ontario passed new laws. The Metropolitan Toronto Regional Conservation Authority was created to manage ravine land and control floods. Thirteen dams were built and people were not allowed to build their houses so close to the rivers. The land along the rivers would be used in future for parks and recreation to prevent such a tragedy from happening ever again.

ABOUT THE AUTHOR

Anne Dublin grew up in Toronto and was a young girl when Hurricane Hazel battered the city. She has lived in Nairobi, Kingston, and Winnipeg where she taught English, French, and library. She now lives in Toronto where she works as a librarian. She keeps busy writing, singing, telling stories, and taking care of her cat, Petunia.

ABOUT THE ILLUSTRATOR

Avril Woodend is finishing her Master's Degree in Landscape Architecture at the University of British Columbia. In the summer, she works as a gardener for the Vancouver Parks Board.

If you liked this book...
you might enjoy these other Hodgepog Books:
read them yourself in grades 3–5,
or read them to younger kids.

Ben and the Carrot Predicament
by Mar'ce Merrell, illustrated by Barbara Hartmann
ISBN 1-895836-54-9   Price $4.95

Getting Rid of Mr. Ributus
by Alison Lohans, illustrated by Barbara Hartmann
ISBN 1-895836-53-0   Price $6.95

A Real Farm Girl
by Susan Ioannou, illustrated by James Rozak
ISBN 1-895836-52-2   Price $6.95

A Gift for Johnny Know-It-All
by Mary Woodbury, illustrated by Barbara Hartmann
ISBN 1-895836-27-1   Price $5.95

Mill Creek Kids
by Colleen Heffernan, illustrated by Sonja Zacharias
ISBN 1-895836-40-9   Price $5.95

Arly & Spike
by Luanne Armstrong, illustrated by Chao Yu
ISBN 1-895836-37-9   Price $4.95

A Friend for Mr. Granville
by Gillian Richardson, illustrated by Claudette
Maclean
ISBN 1-895836-38-7   Price $5.95

Maggie & Shine
by Luanne Armstrong, illustrated by Dorothy Woodend
ISBN 1-895836-67-0   Price $6.95

Butterfly Gardens
by Judith Benson, illustrated by Lori McGregor
McCrae
ISBN 1-895836-71-9   Price $5.95

The Duet
by Brenda Silsbe, illustrated by Galan Akin
ISBN 0-9686899-1-4 $5.95

Jeremy's Christmas Wish
by Glen Huser, illustrated by Martin Rose
ISBN 0-9686899-2-2 $5.95

Let's Wrestle
by Lyle Weis, illustrated by Will Milner and Nat Morris
ISBN 0-9686899-4-9 $5.95

A Pocketful of Rocks
by Deb Loughead
ISBN 0-9686899-7-3 $5.95

Logan's Lake
by Margriet Ruurs, illustrated by Robin LeDrew
ISBN 1-9686899-8-1   Price $5.95

And for readers in grade 1-2,
or to read to pre-schoolers

Sebastian's Promise
by Gwen Molnar, illustrated by Kendra McCleskey
ISBN 1-895836-65-4   Price $4.95

Summer With Sebastian
by Gwen Molnar, illustrated by Kendra McClesky
ISBN 1-895836-39-5   Price $4.95

The Noise in Grandma's Attic
by Judith Benson, illustrated by Shane Hill
ISBN 1-895836-55-7   Price $4.95

Pet Fair
by Deb Loughead, illustrated by Lisa Birke
ISBN 0-9686899-3-0 $5.95